This book belongs to:

_ _ _ _ _ _ _ _ _ _ _ _ _ _ _ _ _ _ _ _

Completely and utterly for Nigel, Maddie, and Charlie Ellis
with my love
K.S.

Sir Charlie Stinky Socks would like to donate 10% of the royalties from the sale of this book to Naomi House Children's Hospice.

EGMONT
We bring stories to life

First published in Great Britain 2007
by Egmont UK Limited
This edition published 2015
The Yellow Building, 1 Nicholas Road
London W11 4AN

www.egmont.co.uk

ISBN (PB) 978 1 4052 7768 6

A CIP catalogue record for this title
is available from the British Library

The Really Big Adventure

Kristina Stephenson

EGMONT

Once upon a time,
there was a **deep, dark forest,**
where monstrous trees groaned,
terrible beasties moaned
and wiggly woos waited
to tickle your toes.

In the middle of the forest,
surrounded by **thorny** bushes,
there stood a tall, tall tower,
with a pointy roof.
At the bottom of the tower
was a big wooden door.

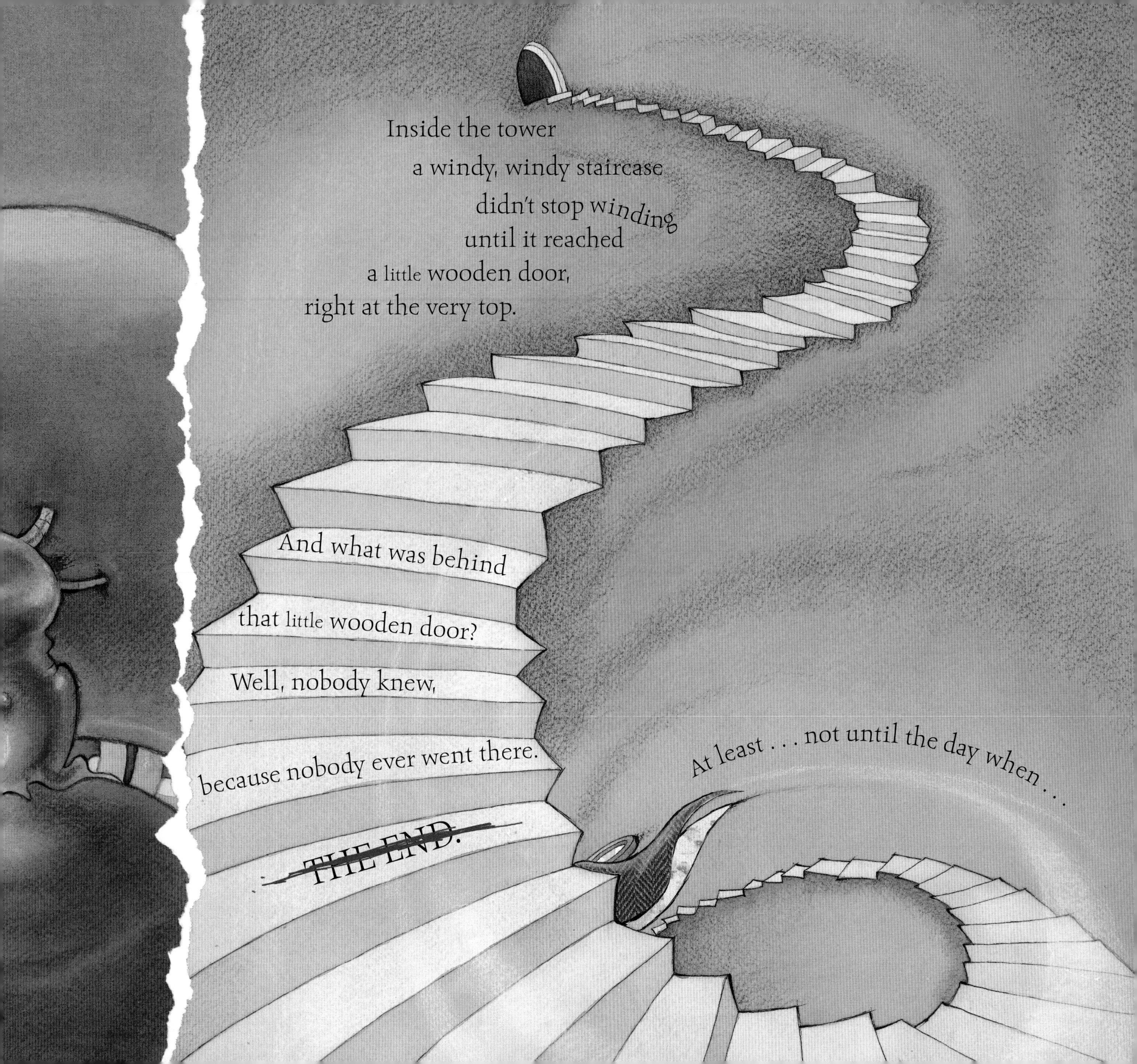

Inside the tower
a windy, windy staircase
didn't stop winding
until it reached
a little wooden door,
right at the very top.

And what was behind
that little wooden door?
Well, nobody knew,
because nobody ever went there.

~~THE END.~~

At least . . . not until the day when . . .

. . . a bold, brave knight,
Sir Charlie Stinky Socks
and his faithful, fearless cat, Envelope,
decided that the time had come for
a really big adventure.

Sir Charlie picked his best sword,
packed some sandwiches,
a big bottle of water and
a favourite little something
for the journey (just in case).

And with a song in his heart
he mounted his good grey mare.

Clip clop,
Clip clop,
Clippety clippety clop!

Over the hills
and far away rode Sir Charlie and his cat.

(Oh, and a wily witch with a watch followed behind on a broom.)

At last they came
to a **deep, dark forest**,
where monstrous trees *groaned*
and **terrible beasties** *moaned*.

Envelope *shivered*.

The good grey mare *quivered*.

(While the witch with
the watch covered her eyes.)

But brave Sir Charlie
stood steady in his boots.

"Sssshhhhhh!" he whispered into the woods.
"'Tis I . . . Sir Charlie Stinky Socks
with a song to *soothe* you."

And as Sir Charlie sang his lullaby
the trees stopped groaning.

But the **terrible beasties**
went on moaning.

"Stop your moaning," cried the knight.
"Come out and eat me if you dare!"

Out of the darkness
crept
six
slobbering
beasties.

That fearless cat, Envelope, scarpered!

The good grey mare fled!

(And even the wily witch
with the watch
trembled behind a tree.)

But bold Sir Charlie did not turn.
Brave Sir Charlie did not run.

Instead he drew his trusty
sword and did what any
good knight would do . . .

. . . he smiled and cut up his sandwiches!

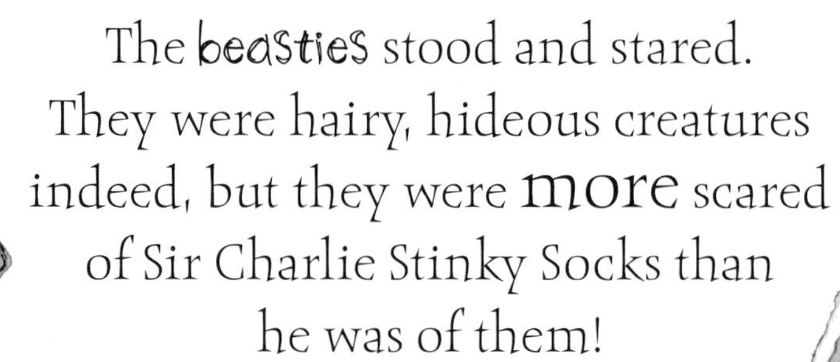

The beasties stood and stared. They were hairy, hideous creatures indeed, but they were more scared of Sir Charlie Stinky Socks than he was of them!

Charlie fed the beasties
and the beasties
stopped moaning.

(And the wily witch
with the watch
looked on with a grin
and checked the time.)

But this was no way to end
a really big adventure.

So Sir Charlie Stinky Socks rescued his cat, rallied his good grey mare
and set off once again, never minding the **wiggly woos** who waited in the grass or
the six *not so* terrible beasties who followed him.

The forest grew **thicker** and the bushes became *thorny*.
Lucky for Envelope and the good grey mare
that Sir Charlie Stinky Socks led the way
with his trusty sword.

Wooshity thwack,
wooshity thwack,
choppity choppity choppity chop!

It was thirsty work for a bold, brave knight;
how glad he was to have a big bottle of water by his side.

And then, at last, they came to
a clearing in the trees
where the sun threw down
its pale yellow light . . .

But it
also threw
its light onto . . .

. . . a long, green dragon!

He was *frightful* and *fearsome*
and coughing out *fire*
while he stomped
in a temper around
the tower.

Ha ha!
thought Sir Charlie Stinky Socks.
Just the thing for a really big *adventure!*

"Stop your roaring, dragon!"
he commanded.

But the dragon did *not* stop.
He went on *coughing* out fire.
He went on *belching* out smoke.
And now his eyes were fixed firmly
on Sir Charlie Stinky Socks.

Was this the end of the line for the bold, brave knight?

Oh my!

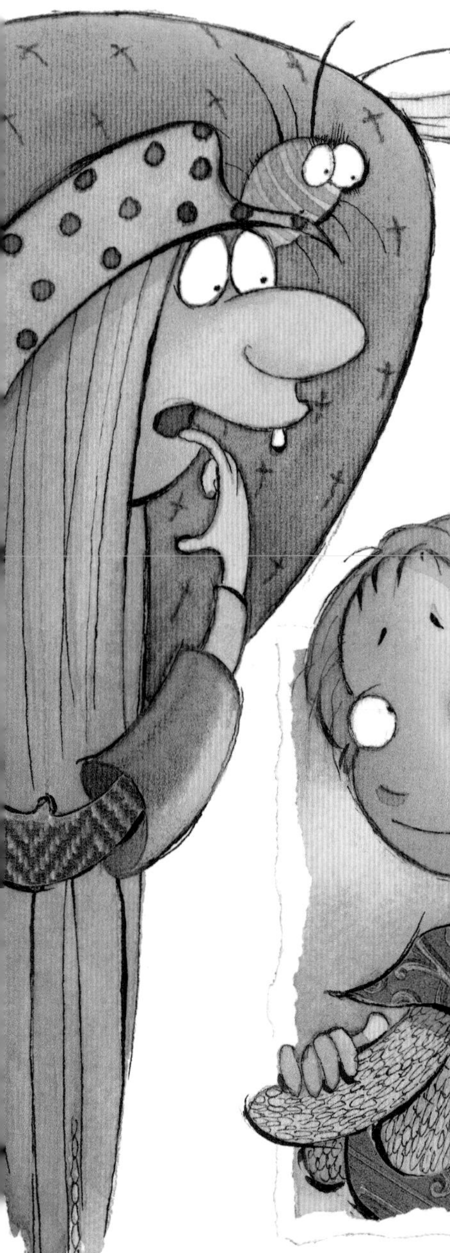

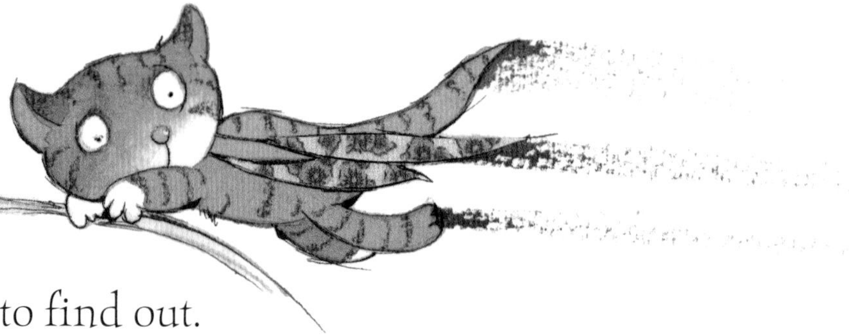

Envelope didn't hang around to find out.
And neither did the good grey mare.

Only a worried, wily witch and a couple of **wiggly woos** watched.

But bold Sir Charlie
did not flinch.

Brave Sir Charlie
did not flicker.

He took out his big bottle
of water and . . .

. . . kind, clever
Sir Charlie Stinky Socks
gave that old dragon
a long,
cooooooool
drink.

"Now you've stopped coughing,"
said the knight to the long, green dragon,
"tell me what's at the top of this tower."

The dragon looked up.
The dragon looked at Sir Charlie.
The dragon scratched
his scaly head and said,
"My dear old thing, I haven't a clue.
It's not a dragon's place to ask,
you know – just – to do."

"Then why don't we find out?"
said Sir Charlie with a grin.

The wily witch took one last look at her watch, jumped for joy and flew off on her broom as Charlie pushed open the **big** wooden door.

Up the *windy, windy* staircase marched Sir Charlie Stinky Socks.
He didn't stop marching until he had taken
his faithful cat, Envelope,
his good grey mare,
six *not so* terrible beasties,
a very curious long, green dragon
and a couple of wiggly woos
right to the very top.

There he opened the little
wooden door and peeped in.

Creeeeeaaaakkkk . . .

A big black cauldron stood in
the middle of the room, and stirring
it was the wily witch (of course).

By her side sat a little princess,
weeping and *wailing*
in a pool of tears.

Sir Charlie looked
at the princess.

Sir Charlie looked at
the bubbling pot.

Sir Charlie didn't wait another minute.
He drew his trusty sword,
and bounded over to rescue
the little princess.

"Stop your weeping!" cried the knight.
**"Sir Charlie Stinky Socks is here
to save you from the pot."**

The witch cackled with laughter.

"I'm not going to cook the *princess*!" squealed the witch.
"I'm cooking the food for her birthday party.
It's today, at three, you see. I do it every year,
you know. I blow up balloons
and decorate the tower.
I send out invitations –
hundreds of them!

And looky here!"
she cried, tip tapping
at the face of
her watch.
"It's nearly three!
Yippee!"

"Then . . . why are you crying, princess?"
asked Sir Charlie.

That night the lights burned brightly
in the tall, tall tower with the pointy roof,
as a happy little princess
had a rip-roaring good time!

"Behold
Sir Charlie Stinky Socks and his friends!"

"Because," shrieked
a *windy, windy* staircase
surrounded by thorns
dragon. And it's in
forest, where wiggly
your toes, hungry
and monstrous
so nobody
ever comes!"

And everyone cheered hooray, **hooray, hooray,**
because that's what people do at the end of
a really big adventure.

When the candles had been blown out and
the cake eaten up, Sir Charlie Stinky Socks took
out the favourite little something he
had brought from home (just in case),
and gave it to the princess.

"Many happy returns of the day!" he said.

the princess, "we live at the top of

in a tall, tall tower with a pointy roof,

and guarded by a *fire-breathing*

the middle of a **deep, dark**

woos wait in the grass to tickle

beasties moan

trees groan . . .

"Oh, yes they do,"

said Sir Charlie, as he

flung open the door.